Coming HOME
from HOME

ALSO BY BRUCE HUNTER

Benchmark (poetry, 1982)

The Beekeeper's Daughter (poetry, 1986)

Country Music Country (stories, 1996)

Coming HOME
from HOME

BRUCE HUNTER

THISTLEDOWN PRESS

Canadian Cataloguing in Publication Data

Hunter, Bruce, 1952–
Coming home from home
Poems.
ISBN 1-894345-11-8
I. Title.
PS8565.U578 C65 2000   C811'.54   C00-920058-4
PR9199.3.H825 C65 2000

Cover photograph courtesy of the Glenbow Museum, Calgary, Alberta.

Typeset by Thistledown Press Ltd.
Printed and bound in Canada

Thistledown Press Ltd.
633 Main Street
Saskatoon, Saskatchewan
S7H 0J8

Canadian   Patrimoine
Heritage   canadien

Thistledown Press gratefully acknowledges the financial assistance of the Canada
Council for the Arts, the Saskatchewan Arts Board, and the Government of
Canada through the Book Publishing Industry Development Program for its
publishing program.

ACKNOWLEDGEMENTS

The author is grateful to the editors of the following in which some of these poems first appeared: *Dandelion*, *Poetry Canada Review*, and *Zymergy*. Several of the poems were short-listed for the CBC/*Saturday Night* Literary Competition in 1997.

"The Night We Tore Up Stanley's Lawn" was chosen as one of the People's Choice poems of 1995 by the *People's Poetry Newsletter* and will be included in *2000% Cracked Wheat* published by Coteau Press. Other poems were included in *90 Poets for the Nineties —An Anthology of American and Canadian Poets* published by The Seminole Press.

The author would like to acknowledge the generous support of Thistledown Press, and its dedication to Canadian writers for more than twenty-five years.

Thanks also to Helen, Ken, Rick and Robert for their ongoing conversations and belief in poetry. And I owe so much to Barry Dempster for his support and editorial suggestions. Finally, if it weren't for Glen Sorestad, so much might never have happened.

Note on the cover photograph

The author's great grandfather and grandmother, Mrs. Robert Anstruther Begg (nee Lavinia Golding), her daughters Norah and Lavinia (the author's grandmother) and her son, Alexander. Dunbow Ranch near Davisberg, Alberta outside High River, circa 1909.

CONTENTS

for Rosemary,
because poetry changed your life
and to the memory of Randy Cloak

O my love, where are they, where are they going
the flash of a hand, the streak of movement, rustle of pebbles.
I ask not of sorrow, but in wonder.
— Czeslaw Milosz, *Bells in Winter*

LIGHT AGAINST LIGHT

I want again to believe
that when we love
we remain
passing always from this light
into the next.

To remember
those X-rays of my lungs
I was shown as a child
whose gauzy shadows
I thought were hidden wings.
You could feel the hot fist of the heart
but where was the soul?

And that his shoulder blades
when Billy stripped by the river
were more than bones
and that we would someday lift our arms.
We had seen the gleaned skeletons
of birds drying on the salt flats.
On each wing, a thumb and four bird fingers.

How we lost faith
and knew that the minister's collar
was a halo that had slipped,
a noose that reddened his face
and made it difficult
for him to look down.

Billy believed
that the 13 loops of the hangman's noose
made a hoop into the next life.
Me, I practised that knot over and over.

But now there's no way back

and at night I ingest the room
and into the room, the building
and into that, the city and the lake,
until I am pulling in
all those edgeless places
where this galaxy becomes another.

Where the mind
is a sail full of light
and the body a vessel.

One day I will keep on going,
borrowed
for a lifetime,
sent spinning back.

That light I was:
all we are
luminous bodies, particles,
one against another
— light against light.

RECURRING DREAMS ON A GARDEN

The garden
— always back to the garden.

And the Dutch gardeners of my dreams:
Billy's father tilling
his velvet loam spilled
against the brome-covered hills of Alberta.

Gleaming white rails of the fence,
a dyke against the drought.
Weeding the intruders:
prairie clover, portulaca, thistle.

Sometimes there is an arbour
dream-borrowed from my parents' yard
with its vines and swinging gate,
hanging on its single rasping hinge.

And then, last night, I am unable to move,
so I wave from this side of the dream.

Billy's father raises a glove,
affable, a man loving his garden,
thinking his way through the rows.

And only when I wake,
rested from its innocence,
do I know why the latch lay closed,
why I can't get there.

Him, seven years dead,
all that time preparing the earth to receive him,
now gone to the green heaven.

TWO O'CLOCK CREEK

All that summer couldn't understand
in the morning as we drove through
dry boulder wash, the matter-of-fact sign nailed
on a creekside spruce:
    TWO O'CLOCK CREEK
    — and no water anywhere.

Me twelve with Uncle John on patrol
in the forestry truck.
Him hungover and with that temper,
you didn't push the obvious.

But that sign taunted me.
As first ranger in the district
he named things factually like an explorer:
Abraham flats after a Stony chief
The map men kept that one,
thinking it Biblical and it was, in a way.

But each afternoon, driving back, sure enough
at two o'clock, there was a creek
roaring cold under the wheels.

Finally, a week before school and the city, I asked,
a prairie boy baffled by the magic of water
appearing anywhere, and on time.
John smirks, swings the Ford
into the ditch and around,
a madman on his way to a holy place.

I hang on as we climb, boulders boil in the fenders.
Double-clutching down into first
onto a horsetrail, then straight up on foot,

a pika whistling at us. Beginning to wish
I hadn't asked about that sign.

Over the alpine meadows
a plateau where mountain sheep startle
at the two of us covered in dust.
He draws his pipe across the foot of a glacier
tipped from the distant sky, a white glory
scooped into the sunslope
in a sheltered cowl of rock.
John points to a green waterfall
spilling over the lip.

Here sky meets land
and water is hard as rock this high
and liquid ice to the tongue and our aching feet.
Where all the rivers begin,
the Whitegoat, the Bighorn
after the sheep behind us.
Headwaters of the upper Saskatchewan
I knew from schoolroom maps,
coursing down to Hudson Bay
with canoes full of coureur de bois.

Below us, blonde grass riffles on Kootenay Plains,
clouds jam the chute the weather comes through
where the Kootenay descended to barter the Cree.
Up here the wind howls cold.

And I saw how a few hours of daylight
warms the ice to a trickle that becomes a torrent
in the glacier's pit. The mystery of rivers

is that they come from somewhere
between earth and sky.
wrung by the sun from clouds and wind.

But when night comes, Two O'clock Creek sleeps,
the waterfall waits frozen, and all the years
since I learned how rivers are made,
this is the place I come to in my dreams
between the highest point of land and the sky,
so I can drink from the clouds.

THE VICAR'S MONDAY

Everything good was English
and hyphenated.
The vicar Pryce-Jones
smelling of briar
and India ink
in an Austin-Healey
with signal arms in the roof pillars
that leapt out on turns.

My grandmother the parish clerk
sent me with him on his Monday rounds
to this widow and another
in the smallest hamlets of the diocese.
His collar clacking open
over sweaty vestments
always fastened
before ascending the next stairs.

Balanced on sprung seats
with an ice cream bribe
while the vicar missed Cambridge common
and cursed the Canadian summer.
Over roads where wolf willow
and mullen lined the ditches.
In the sunroof
came the breath of pinesmoke and fir
sage and dust off the grassy dunes
that met the mountains.

I learned to hate
what was good,
the studied and pious lore.

Whatever was raw
and green, I loved.
And when the new man came
from Regina,
he went to the river
and slipping the bark
of the damp willow,
he carved a whistle —
its scream sleek and shrill,
native as a cougar.

SAVAGE STONES

All the streets of our town
seemed littered
with the homemade weapons of my brothers.
Slingshots and catapults
warring on invisible enemies
from behind the buttresses of our tall green fence
that favoured daydreams of a fortress.

All the alleys then
seemed peopled by bullies or mad dogs
and my brothers ventured forth like a single weapon,
two savage stones,
tethered in a Y of cord,
half lariat, half sling,
a bolas sent hurling
with twin velocity around the neck
or leg of prey.

All their days
spent stalked or imagined stalking,
and because like deer know hunting season
or fish the shadow of a rod,
my brothers' quarry knew them.

They bagged nothing
but the nodding green Goliath
of a goose-necked streetlamp
and for years
that bolas hung there, clacking
like a stone bell

over the heads of my brothers
who had long moved on
to finer weapons.

WHEN LOVE WAS A FIST

My father was handy with his hands
and a sucker for scrap.
A man who'd done hard time,
hard labour.
Determined we'd not do the same.
All seven of us.

And my grandmother who'd swoop through
on her Saturday morning visits.
A white-gloved general,
my mother hated,
inspecting the barracks.

I learned, years later,
she held the mortgage
and when my parents divorced,
sold their house
but that's another story.

One day she found
the Black Doctor
as we called it,
my father's invention,
a brute with his hands.
A man who made garages
and extra rooms for the houses we lived in.

With those same snips
he cut a man loose from a wreck,
he made a handle
and then a paddle like a cricket bat
from the thick rubber

used as baseboards in hospitals
and jails.
A tool to fix us when we broke.

I don't remember him strapping us
only my grandmother's voice
when she discovered it
and the latches used to lock us in our rooms.

I don't remember him ever using it
though he did
because I remember its sting, its weight,
and the fear
that controlled us long after that
as we waited in our rooms —
every creak of his floor
and wobble in his stairs
as he descended.

He was afterall
better with snips than a hammer,
a tinsmith not a carpenter
and for that we were glad,
what he might have made of wood.

I want to tell you though
it was another time
and that my father, with this mother
and without the father you may have had
and the life he'd been given,
tried to make sense of it.

And we all called it love.

RAGE

" . . . the way people use language makes me furious. The ones who reject the colloquial & common culture. The ones who on the one hand laud the common and denigrate the intellect, as if we are not thinking . . . It takes us nowhere . . . "

— Erin Mouré, *Furious*

"I'm afraid of my male rage,
this growing thing, this buddy, this
shadow, this new self, this stranger . . .
— Pier Giorgio di Cicco, *Flying Deeper Into the Century*

Hollow men indeed
our gullets empty as gulleys —
without wombs
we fill ourselves with rage
 — swelling proudly.

Piling into our cars one night
because Marnie's boyfriend struck her —
racing across town
in our rage, this madness
until one by one, we slowed down
and somebody pulled over.

What each of us wouldn't admit:
pounding some sense into him
wouldn't have helped at all.

And the paunch is a lonely scream —
no place for it but our bodies
and we want to take it out, away
but we stagger on,

our belts sagging under its weight
— our potbellies glowing hubcaps
on the wheels of the body.

What we are left with —
without weapons, we beat ourselves bigger
and bigger, if there's no one else in the way —
what it means, I don't have
the damndest, but by the time it matters
in the fourteen floors of the seniors' building
there are only three of us left.

ALIBIS

There in the rogue's gallery
on the paper's back page
that sallow glare
where you see nothing
but your darker self.
A swastika tattooed into the forehead
with a prison shank.
The dogged face.
But then
everyone there looks like family,
even Charles Manson.

*Once, you say, I found my hands
around the neck of a woman I loved
or said I did,
not knowing what I was doing.
My hands did. She did.
She ran.*

*She called me back,
took my hands:
More, she said.
And I've been running ever since.*

All your clever alibis
can't explain him away —

or all the I-love-you's, so much
I want you, dead
or alive.

LILACS

They were not
those mauve and lavender-scented
that suckered
around the window of my parents' bedroom
on the prairies.
Growing everywhere
those dry clustered pods
warning like rattlesnakes
in the wind.
More seed than flower.

Ours were the light and Japanese lilacs
that bloomed
at the window
of the first place we rented,
a basement room.
It was a summer of firsts
so we thought.

We had no vases
but the bedroom was filled
with jars of lilacs,
leaves growing underwater,
green fish, white moons.
And the scent that now belongs to light.

The taste of sage
on your neck.
Lilacs and footprints
in the hot bare dust,
all that's left.

One summer,
the old waft of light,
enough to remember
too much to desire.

WHEN WE WERE LOVERS

I wanted to be Italian
to change my name to Di Cicco
or Pavese; I learned
to drink cappuccino,
acquired a taste for pesto,
women in Florentine leathers,
chic hats and seamed stockings
in the Cafe Roma.
None of this was difficult.

And my Jamaican friend
looks amused when I explain
how the Scots and the Irish hate the English
— and the English hate everyone else —
all the shades of white.
He thought we all looked the same.

My Anglo friends want to be Italian too.
When all we have
is the man in the Irish Spring commercial
in a tweed cap
and of course, Prime Minister Muldoon.

But now I'm confused
if it was you or the romance
of olive trees and a Mediterranean skin
always darker than mine,
a language more capable of rage.

Mine is the lost tongue
of my uncles, their bagpipes,
the beat of a battle hymn
four hundred years ago.

But how wrong I was
for each day my blood darkens
with new rage for this.
And the only word I remember now
in Italian
is *ciao*.

MANTA RAY

In Kensington Market
between the greengrocer's
truck, bottomed out
with over-ripe pineapples
and the cheeseman's
bagel-steamed front,
the fishmonger's boy
carries it
arms' length from his chest
stacked onto milk crates
while a crowd gathers.

An odd cross between a shark
and home plate,
the supple razor of its tail
coiled in broken mangoes.
A hacksaw grin
that widens as rigor mortis sets in
and the grey skin buckles and dries.
The eyes pale sunken figs
that the wasps warm to
where someone has inserted —
one bent forward,
another tilted outward
— red horns of pimento.

Oh love,
to think once I saw you
feathered and vain.
How you loved a crowd,
the flash of your teeth.
No bird
but second cousin to a shark.

FRIENDS

Three years since the divorce,
pulled between the arcane and obvious,
tragic or comic,
or the 90s,
I'm never sure anymore.

But it's Saturday night
and I'm standing
stretched in the windows
of my ex-wife's new apartment.
She is cooking dinner.
We are, as it goes, just friends.

The man she's in love with
has also just moved,
across the road,
waiting for the final decree.
He's got the kids this weekend.
Why she's seeing me.

And here I am
silhouetted in the window
with a hammer
putting up blinds, a husband again.

I can see him
and his two kids in the park.
He nods to me.
Nice people, we are.
Which is the problem.
I don't want to be good at this.

Knowing that when I leave,
and the kids,
the two of them make love.

And the woman I've been seeing
is home tonight
waiting for the call
from her husband's lawyer.

SEPTEMBER ROSES

Summer's last.

A man
and woman fucking
with hard bodies
in the strange cold heat
of the last years of the century.

A gathering
to carry us
into the next millennium.

And on the balcony
the silvered buds
red and frosted as nipples.

PICKING APPLES

Not Northern Spies,
nor Granny Smiths. Yours
Plump Russets
rouged and weighty.
Or whatever.

When I learned to pick apples, two-handed
in the Niagara orchards,
weighing them in my palms,
the old orchardman showed me.
Letting gravity do its trick.
Lifting them away.

Their ripe and wondrous falling.
Their stems curled, a small leaf
fluttering like a sprouted wing.
Lowering them into the canvas
cradled on his chest.

And I had no idea then
he was talking about you,
or about love.

SLOW TRAIN HOME

We take our grief
from the new city to the old;
Montreal, St. Denis,
a carriage up cobbled hills.
Too soon yet for the boulevard cafes
but so little it takes to warm us.

Cafe au lait in hot bowls
steaming in our faces.
Notre Dame, a thousand candles
reeking of piety
under the statues of women martyrs
carved of old pine.

Rocking us homeward
shunted onto and off the main line
waiting out the long freights.
Your eager arms, ardent kisses.
Your body breaking open
and I'm gaping into it,
where that child was
we made one day at dawn.

Our bodies pressing, the train below
shaking us now
and the child somehow not dead
but passed back into us
where we warm it in our arms.

The slow train home,
starwash, rods of lupine frosty
by the stacked ties.
Leftover moon on the tables of the club car.
Others all sleeping.

We make love there
not out of daring but because we must.
The need to smash the body
back into molecules,
mesh with the stippled grasses
and muddied fields.

And dawn, the first green rain.
Innumerable moons implode in the window
with soft gasps of light.
Moving us from the old
into the new.
This terror
and all the cold new air.

DECEMBER ARSON IN CABBAGETOWN
(for Andrew Wreggett)

Allure, always
both soft and metallic,
like sex
like a steel blade against the throat,
like a hammer and a nail
ticking against the fillings of our teeth.

As much as we love
one so differs from another
that there can be no universal wisdom,
no True North of the Heart,
no magnetic field that points us
heartward
homeward.

But always that one True Thing
we are, finally,
always, always alone with our lost allure
ticking like a blade
or a bomb.

And sitting in a donut shop on Parliament Street
December 24 a few years ago,
reading your letter " . . . She left . . . "
This much we know,
but instead, I want to make you laugh.

Like, love is a donut:
when she's eaten the rest
and left you the hole.
But serious business, this angst,
this love stuff that can kill us.

And besides it's thirty below,

the pathetic fallacy not mine,
but an arsonist's
who torched the house
across the street last night.

And the firemen still lumber through the ruins,
in frozen yellow jackets,
ravaged timber steaming into black crystal
and for a raw moment

I see the clarity of ruins
and like our mutual friend, Camus,
I am shivering, breathless
in the presence of such beauty.

SARDINIA
(as told by Margaret)

Ours was a Cold War love.
Stationed on the Pine Tree,
second defence to the DEW Line,
south of Saskatoon in the grassy hills,
a stretch of radar domes,
like igloos across the near north.

We lived in the officers' compound,
I went back there once, just to see.
Nothing left now but loops of asphalt
where the trailers butted into the hillsides.

My husband in those long Saskatchewan nights,
told of Sardinia, his first posting.
And those Mediterranean girls
with their darker skin. Names he called out
as he reached for me in his sleep.

And we played cards:
kitchens and living rooms full of smoke.
With other couples, always officers and their wives,
none of us unmatched, as we bowled in the two-lane alley
next to the officers' mess.
All the codes of dress and decorum.
And I never suspected a thing.

Worked down in the county office typing.
While he took swing shifts in the radio tower,
that's now a shell on the hill, the white dome gone.
Eavesdropping on the talk of Soviet pilots
and our own in the high Arctic.
A man who'd read Chekhov in the Russian.

The day the cat smelled of perfume

it all came together
as it fell apart.
When her husband mentioned to her
mine had requested a transfer to Sardinia,
and she broke down, told him everything.

And my husband, trained in code
and cyphers, the man I thought I knew, stayed silent.
All those secret glances, the double entendres he loved
— the pokerface.

All the reasons she told me later, I've forgotten,
but not her red eyes,
the stain of my slap spreading on her cheek,
and I hugged her like a sister,
my nose in that damned perfume of hers.

TEMPTATION AND DESIRE — BANFF, 1985

You talk and talk.
Long past what you know
the woman waiting for you back home
and this woman's husband would ever understand.
Walking outside the lives you have briefly left behind.

Like you're seventeen,
though you're not. Neither of you.
This time with none of the disadvantages.
But somehow the talk is too good.
And the river below
spotted with glacial ice and powdered rock.
So fast it carries scree from the canyon.

You're aware of the hairs
on each other's arms. You know
a danger greater than the drop below.
You brush close on the trail
that passes out of town into the black woods.
There are few stars tonight, many clouds
and no moon. You wander blind,
following the noise of the river.
You hear the echo of the canyon beside your feet.

And you know the old possibility of metaphor
is that it leaps between the known
and the unknown. Here the leap is as small
as the fall is great. And you're hopelessly old-fashioned
both of you, you've talked, but you know
that one movement always produces another
unseen, unheard. And whether or not
the philosopher's old tree is seen falling,
it hits another and another.

Your breath steams in the alpine air.
You follow each other's voices,
the heat of her back. So much desire
and complication. Her children, your wife.

And you're here to write,
but not about this, which leads you back
into these woods every time
and this dangerous traverse. The others
back in town in bars
looking for this. What they will do to know it.
It could be that simple,
but it's not, it never was.

So you drop over stumps, blind roots,
your teeth clamp down hard when you misstep.
You know where this could go, but won't.
Not because you're noble,
nor wise,
memory reminds you.

When the trail drops off to the falls,
you halt there, your pupils large,
figuring on the moon behind the clouds.
So much, so little of it yours.
White thunder of the falls in your ears,
scent of juniper
and oh, what little
you need to see.

SEASONS OF THE CITY

Between sunrise and moonset,
beach and watermark, between
quadrants, north and south
between jazz and more jazz, smoke
and fire, hail and snow, portentous
and sublime, between rain and lightning,
subterfuge and centrifuge, between buckeyes
and sumach, between Bathurst
and Tecumseh.

All the seasons of the city,
between the sated and starved — the malnourished
die content and the conservatives
enjoy their steaks only if others are hungry.
Between the bread and the circus, between Baudelaire
and Bachelard — the spaces of the spaced
on night, on the speed of light.

Between the pious and the pitied, between
a curse and a prayer; my God,
it's not the commitment that counts
it's the tone.

Between darkness and light-blindness, between
dead and dying, grieving and aggrieved,
born and bearing, spinning with the seasons.
Like that dream of my youth
dizzy with vertigo from the spinning planet;
without pull, I'm earth-freed,
space bound, out of gravity
beyond fear.

And I awoke always, I swear,
having touched the ceiling
my lungs full of light.

NEAR ST. JAMESTOWN CEMETERY

All night in the arms of the city
watching the man
who spins swans and reindeer
out of torched glass,
snipping and tying
as the street goes by.

Seven o'clock the moon comes out
with the sleek girls in angora and leather
beside the pretty boys in their white jeans —
legs arced from the curb.

When the gardener closes the iron gates
the cats arrive, their furred backs
of smoke, ginger and calico,
tails snapping as they whip around the cemetery
dozens more on every headstone.

Darkness and the cars already begin to slow
and the gawkers lean over balconies,
the bars begin to smoke
and oh, the glory of,
the cops slouched waiting
because what could go wrong
will, soon enough.

MY STREET

Here on this fabulous street
where I am never alone, the deaf man,
not the dumb man, wired,
my ears full of microphones:
the tick of streetcars tracking by
as a crowd gathers to enter
the fantastic purple walls of a night club.

But the show begins in the street
when Katie the barker yells:
"cock, fuckass, police"
and a man in black leather
with a steel hook for a hand
spears an apple for his girlfriend.

And between the tattoo parlour
where the bikers drill their arms
with skulls and daggers
and the window of Sister Waneita, Reader of Stars
where a tiger tabby crouches among the snake plants,
a man who resembles Karl Marx directs traffic
and curses the buses that roar back
while Jimmy and his pal Roberto
race electric wheelchairs down opposite sides of the street.

And the Portuguese huddle to mass
while a fat hooker drops into an expensive Ford
and a shirtless man driven towards somewhere
slamdances into the crowd that parts for him
as Gibson the blind guy peddles sunglasses
and whistles at all the girls
and yells: "Baby, I can *smell* you're beautiful."

And a man with no legs
knuckles his way on a wheeled board
then tucks it and ascends the stairs
with a swagger that has legs
into the Galaxy Donut Shop
to drink with the man with no arms
who upends a cup with his teeth.

And the beautiful man who plays guitar
with a withered hand,
the women buy his poetry as he blesses them.
On this street, the droolers laugh
at the scab-armed girl who burns herself
and she laughs back.
The cleft argue with the mute in furious wet sputters.
When we greet you on my street
we look for your wires
your scars.

PISSING OUTDOORS

This is the Ralph Lauren piss,
the designer leak.

Because the first privy
was the invention of an Englishman.
Some will insist it was the suggestion
of a woman. Others
claim it is yet another example
of the oppression of women.

All this shirking indoors.
Among the men I know
there is an intimate story told —
a Masonic handshake, of sorts.

The great outdoors
whether from the top floor
or between the cars of a moving train.
Mundanely, from overpasses,
in phone booths, woods, from mountaintops,
diving towers, or window washer's booms
high above the crowds.

Yesterday I saw a businessman
step into a corner off King and Bay
with a sure step
that suggests this is regular.

Or the guy from the phone company
who outside a bar one sub-zero night
joined a group
showering the body of a shiny new Cadillac.

And any man who denies it
is the first to duck into the bushes
when no one's looking.
The golden arc
that returns us to the earth.

Namewriting in the snow —
something at last women can not do
or want to —
something of our own,
the glory of a pisser, a piss-up.

Small boys playing firemen
around a campfire.
Such useful things. All of us
with our rainmakers.

THE BRIDE OF BAY

Finally, that first cracking day of spring.
A full-time job and payday
and tomorrow, a haircut and some clothes,
almost bourgeois.

Heading downtown
in my favourite old sweater
to find the first vendor
who sprongs his umbrella
like a curbside crocus
in a town where spring
is a roasted hot dog right from the cart
with extra onion and hot mustard on poppyseed.

Too early for the Blue Jays, I settle to consider
the sad ornithological order
in front of old city hall.
Wrens waggle their pert bums
as they nip off crumbs of bun, flinging them backwards
over their heads, those showoffs,
until the pigeons bump them
and then the gulls squatter in
and a mad-haired panhandler flaps them all away
as he commands the fountains to rise and fall
as coins are thrown in a box at his feet.

And the wind makes kites out of everything
and newspapers ride the updraft on Bay Street
wrapping themselves like obscene dogs
 around businessmen's legs.
No more perfect use for the *Globe* than this.

And me warming in the pale sun
and the benches around the fountain
filled with the like-minded, warming their hands

around steaming cups.
Sure, there'll be another snowstorm,
but in two weeks the Jays open
and it's finally spring in Upper Canada.

Which is just fine
until I drop my keys in the trashbasket
along with my napkin.
With the help of gravity they are on the bottom.
The basket is very full of things
neither I nor anyone wants
except for of course my keys.
And it is, as I said, windy.
So I find a wire used to bundle newspaper
and begin to fish
somewhat earlier than I'd planned.

Soon I've sent a string
of garbage windward on Bay
hooking only a Coke can and a pair of pantyhose,
wondering how she did that in front of city hall.

I'm considering climbing in
when I realize I have an audience:
the wrens and their lurid bird giggles
while odder birds move in for a handout.
Decent people stare and now I'm head bird
in a flock that includes my friend
who circles me in glee,
flapping his arms.

Finally, I hook them, slightly mustardy
and I have to say — but deeply relished.
And as I turn windblown, a lot sheepish

and tattered, one of the decent folk,
a woman with good perfume, one of those
whose gloves guard the collection plate at church,
presses a ten into my hand
and before hurrying off says:
"Son, buy yourself a nice meal."

And I walk fast down Queen
that ten burning my hand
hotter than all the money I've ever made
and the bum chasing me
takes it gladly and shreds it,
stands with expensive confetti in his hair
at the corner of Business and Queen
grinning like a bride.

WHAT MY STUDENTS TEACH ME

Federico
tells me it's too cold here
but some choice.
You go out one morning,
the car hood's open a little;
three sticks of dynamite
and this is the third time.
In Salvador you take the hint:
you leave.

Ginny Fung
writes of the love
of her and her husband.
The first English she learned
was curses.
Those faces
she could read
in any language.

Cyrous
on the most profound moment of his life
writes a vague tribute
to world harmony and brotherhood.
When I question it,
he says
I am a Baha'i from Iran.
This is for my friends,
not wanting me to seem foolish.
I nod dumbly as he explains
he was made to watch
as the blades fell
and their heads dropped in the street.

Leong Hiu
who now signs her name Lisa
has not seen her brother
since the night
the pirates boarded in the China Sea,
tells me she likes the winter here
because when she wakes
all the white stars are lying on the ground.

Shatha
tells the class
I am visiting my mother after work
babysitting my sister's children
when the sirens went.
We hid under the table
covering my nieces with our bodies
as the bombs fell the teapot shattered.
Everything crashing, it seemed forever.
You were watching that night
on your televisions: Desert Storm.

Dan
says it began in April.
Two million of us sir,
in the Square, I was so proud to be Chinese.
I was a reporter
when the official came into the office
and said, *no more stories!*
I was so angry I quit.
When the tanks came in June
 — we ran, hearing the screams,
too scared to look back.
Now I can no longer write, I study computers.

Fardad
speaks of a trip to the front with his friend
who asked to drive.
We stopped for water.
I was gone a minute.
When I came out,
a missile, there was nothing left.
At the court martial, his mother screamed at me,
I should have been in his place.

And me,
what do I know.
I am a man on the beach
where the boats come in.

WHAT I KNOW ABOUT GERALD

That Gerry, the name the others called him,
was too joyful for his dignity.
That he was quiet and given to days of rage
when everything was dark.

That he was the only student
who ever told me I was wise
the day we talked about spirits
and how the earth was a holy mother.
That he was grey and moustached, older than all the others.
That his fierceness was a necessary force to live by.

That he kept trying when the others failed.
That he was an Ojibwa from somewhere north of here.
That he loved the Jamaican woman in heels
who showed her cleavage and said I'm not ashamed.
That he laughed and said neither am I.

That when I called the counsellor back all I had was scraps.
That she told me he was a roomer
in a place where no one knew him.
That somewhere he had a sister no one could find.
That he had tried twice before.

That he had a small bundle of possessions
and nowhere to send them.
That when he went down to Scarborough Bluffs
the spirit welcomed him.
That the waters of Lake Ontario consumed him.

That whatever wisdom I have is not enough.
That his grey eyes follow me as I watch my classes
for the watery arms that took him.

51

PROGNOSIS

Eight days before Christmas
and three weeks before the invasion of Iraq,
in a waiting room in Mount Sinai hospital.
"Is it serious?" I ask the nurse.
"No," she says, but I know she's lying.

Seven others wait with me. All of us afraid for our eyes.
Mine blur with drops. One by one,
the specialist examines us.
"Fine, fine," he says. "You are free to go."

My turn and he pulls back my eyelids.
Uncomfortable, he disappears.
I am called to another room.
A camera lens is pressed to my pupils.

My head rocks with incoming bolts of light
that move faster and stronger, through my eyes
and around my skull wired with electrodes.
My nails dig into the hard chair.
Tears soak my chin.

"Don't blink," the nurse says.
"I'll tell you anything you want to know," I joke.
My eyes flare with trapped light.
The office has no shape.
Everything melts, foreshadowing.

She tells me the medical term
for something I've always had,
unknown in North America, epidemic in Finland,
none of which matters anyway
because there's no cure
and the prognosis is always
that our leaving begins
as soon we are born.

And that likely mine began a thousand years ago
with a Finnish sailor and a Scottish thrall
who passed it to their children
and the New World and now
in the small separations of my retina,
the slow implosions that will come
one day to pure light,
as my body deserts me.

And I promise you, I'm going,
but not into darkness.
When sight fades,
vision always gets sharper: your shape
and the distance between us.
One thing becomes everything,
light into light.

THOSE LIGHTS

11 floors up or 30
a single light
at 2 AM or 5,
all the lonely numbers.

One wakes up
dreaming the job he used to do,
his fist on a phantom wheel.
The wind calling him back
to those roads he ploughed.
Such snow!
But here in the night
too many streets
he can't get through.

Another paces her room,
sleep shafted.
And she was just getting back to it,
in that haunted calm before dawn.
Twelve years since he stepped out
without his hearing aid.
Didn't see the train coming, she was told.

Suddenly, there he was again,
and the ache,
walking with her one more time
before he veered off
to wherever they go
in our dreams.
Where nothing ends.
Not that body of his. Nor the dream
that wakes us shivering,
snow on our tongues.

And this life
always elsewhere.
Someday we'll sleep.
For now
what to do with these hands,
this body.

SKYHOOKS

And now, mid-week, mid-life,
with my brothers and their children
in the foothills above the city of our birth.
With our bright skyhooks — a name
better saved for these kites:
a skyful of flying ruckus
in the reckless wind
off the Rockies — a red box,
a flying blue carp and fighting dragon tails.

Each of them angling for light,
strung between existence and dream
trolling for skyfish or errant angels
lost in the lure of the clouds.

Thirty years past,
my first job and that apprenticeship
 — how I went to the foreman
when they sent me off to find
that mythical tool — the skyhook,
every apprentice sent chasing,
like left-handed monkey wrenches, queafy tape
or scurpan dimmers
 — while the journeymen guffawed.
But my father's stories warned me.

Told the foreman I wasn't going back
until I had one
and we made up a box
and a bill of lading, labelled it boldly.

The journeymen stood big-eyed
as boys, wanting to believe.
No one had ever come back with one.
Maybe there *was* a skyhook afterall.

Until the box torn open
revealed a rod I'd bent into a question mark
with a loop on the end
and disappointed, they chased me
for playing the joke backwards.
And here, now on a windy hill,
so much behind us, my brothers softer now
than our father, the future has come for us.

Deep sky above, the laving of prairie below.
In our hands the sorcery of strings
summoning fishes and loaves, whatever we want,
the old stories we've almost lost:
all the possibilities of belief
and sky.

SOURCES

Playing on a Y of willow
or iron rebar or bent coat hanger,
whether it's a cup of water
or a river
it's always the same tensile tune
pitched high in his ears.

Because, he told me
the water dowser's strung
like a gut
between the air
and the secret rivers below.

He tells of his mother's torment:
sleepless for years
and when he dowsed her bedroom
below her pillow
rushed an ancient and subterranean river
that near yanked the bar
from his hands.

All those years the family laughed at her
convinced that the brain
knows better than her nocturnal ear,
that same ear he'd been god-given.

THE NIGHT YOU DIED

You passed through one last time
and though I've seen ghosts all my life
I almost didn't believe it,
thought it memory's way
of keeping the present for the future
as poetry is the heart's reckoning with reason.

But the room cooled suddenly
and your presence woke me —
you were on your way home, somewhere
and it was urgent
that you pass through one more time,
that I see you.

Though I still didn't completely believe —
but you had one last thing to show me.
Later, I lay awake thinking of the time
I dared Charlie I could find water
— it's bullshit, I said,
hoping it would fail,
though I knew of electrical fields
between water and the body.
I've studied too much science
to completely disbelieve.

We found a willow fork,
though he told me a crowbar
would work just as well,
and we found water
and I became a sceptical disbeliever.

And when you passed through
I wanted to believe this was memory
dealing with itself,
not that tug

between the arms and body of the dowser,
the water and clay.

Pliant as willow, taut
as the line between
the trout we never caught
and the heart that hoped we would,
a force field pulling me back into the earth
between belief and disdain,
holy terror and exaltation.

It had to be you
and when I slept finally
my dreams were trout streams
leaping with light.

THE SCOTTISH GRANDMOTHERS

And the long ago love of them,
stomping from the bus stop
with their Hudson's Bay shopping bags
of cinnamon buns. Their little houses
smelling of broth and camphor.

Their calfskin Bibles
and fishing tackle
in the top of the hall closet,
the only opulence in their dour lives,
root beer fermenting from things
gathered on the prairie — an old world recipe
that exploded once or twice, glass in everyone's
shoes, among the pious names of the prophets
passed from Bible to children, the psalms
and epiphanies slightly scented
of root beer.

Those small defiant women
whose generosity came from austerity,
one of them rolling her smokes,
"Hell, cheap? We were poor.
And your Aunt Maggie wrote:
Cold here — don't come.
I did anyway."

And whatever gifts given them at Christmas
always returned to the sender at birthdays
or other Christmases.
Not a white glove among them,
their chin hairs and eyebrows
never tweezed until the undertaker got them.
Their stories come back in mine

— all the long lines of the Scottish grandmothers
bearing teaboxes of shortbread
over legendary hills of gorse and heather,
the wind scented always
of cinnamon and root beer.

MEDITATIONS ON
THE IMPROBABLE HISTORY OF A SMALL TOWN

Hate Teacher Convicted Again
July 17, 1994

Midway between Red Deer
and Rocky Mountain House on Highway 11.
Eckville pop. 800
and Jim Keegstra.
Former auto mechanic, former
school teacher, now auto mechanic again.

The original settlers recognizing potential
in the belly above the Bible belt
called it Hell
under their breath.
Grasshoppers, drought,
and mosquitoes
when it finally did rain.

But it's not the kind of name
that goes on a CPR map
in a fine new country.
What about Heck, someone offered.
Too obvious said another.
Someone else: Heckville.
A remittance man
with a sense of humour,
so the township papers came back
Eckville.

What happened here
happens in every small town.
Some born, some died, most
moved away.

Until a man taught history
the way you rebuild engines:
do a bit here,
drop this, add that
and what you don't have
make yourself. Found himself teaching math:
six million equals zero.
No one saw anything,
not the principal nor the school board.

And when the trial's over
and the reporters go back
to Toronto or Calgary or Tel Aviv,
the principal and the superintendent
still there and the name
Eckville.

Although sometimes
it must be Hell.

THE DAY WE TORE UP STANLEY'S LAWN

The neighbours thought we were crazy.
And so did we.
As the naked clay dried
and the wind off Kalamalka Lake
swirled it in our faces.

And the bare lines of the irrigation pipe
lay like a grid on a brown map
of the West,
the windy West, the West of twenty year droughts,
the West that was never green,
where hard pan is dry ten feet down.

The neighbours came to watch
and a police car stopped by
— he'd had a complaint
but there's no law against tearing up your lawn.

Drinking Stanley's beer until dusk
sitting on the mounds of dying sod
we started on the dinner's wine
and stared at each other,
began pulling up the plastic grid.

Brass nozzles fell on the driveway,
black pipe curled around us
and we whooped
and Stanley the iron man yanked hard
and we both pulled.
We'd caught something,
so we tugged again
and up came a man who'd been watering his driveway
and there were three of us now
and Stanley's wife and kids,
we all pulled hard

and heard a distant rumble,
as lights went off around the lake
— we'd bagged the dam
and freed the river.

All night it went on
and that one went down to free another
and another, over the Great Divide,
the Brazeau, the Oldman, the Whitegoat.

Lights went off all over the Northwest,
as the Columbia, the Cascade,
the San Fernando, the Colorado,
down along the Great Divide,
rivers smacking down the squatter's shacks,
and their kidney-shaped pools
and all the putting greens of Arizona.

Everywhere people came out to watch
the rivers come back.

"We've started something," Stanley said.

We waited,
wondering what next,
and perfected a new sport,
whirling it high and around us,
tossing the lawnmower over our heads
like a four-wheeled caber.

And all around our feet
there was new growth:
sweetgrass, brome,
fescue and wild rose.
The earth began to smell again
the day Stanley pulled the plug.

We'd broken the green spell
that Eastern green, that English curse.
And the new colours now:
yellows, the gold of palomino,
of sundogs, greys and adobes.

Hoofbeats we heard one night.
"No," Stanley said,
but I heard them too
and the sky fluttered
dark with birds coming back
and the earth shook.

And all the impatient farmers returned
to the green and possible East,
and the Impossible West was quiet and golden again.
No pump jacks, no farms,
the West the way it was.

And Stanley's new lawn spread
like a tumbleweed blowing across the West
the Northwest, the Southwest,
the golden West.

And now the wind blows,
light as prairie clover,
sweet as sage.

THE TOMB AT DUNN

I found him that day I walked down Eighth Avenue,
a month after my grandmother's funeral,
past the Glenbow, and remembered in her time
it was called Stephen Avenue
when the sandstone buildings
and the gaslights ranged to the prairies.

"Begg," I asked the archivist,
her eyes averted. Everyone claims family here.
Nothing left I thought, of the loquacious family
my great-great grandfather
who wrote *A History of British Columbia*.

But she came back, six boxes of letters,
two hundred items of clothing and tools from the ranch,
his poetry and maps, photographs and diaries:
"I've left my native land forever.
I fear I shall not see her again."

His handwriting changed with the voyage
and after weeks of seasickness:
"I am overjoyed to see
the cliffs of Quebec City, my new home."

His notes on the pictures,
guide me now to the northeast coast,
above the 68th parallel, Finland and Norway over there.

Coming home to Caithness, where in the pubs
Canada's still a distant dream of wilderness and Indians,
one hundred and sixty years
after my great-great-grandfather sought it
and I've followed him back across the sea.

On the road to John O'Groats and the Orkneys,
we find the village of Watten and the Brown Trout

where the farmers drink.
Our last night before we go home to Canada,
a name we now hear as adventure.

"Begg," one local says, "means small in Gaelic."
"And square," another snorts, "low to the land."
"And hairy," a shaggy one nods.
They laugh, stout furry men themselves, a Scottish gale
whines outside, everything low in this treeless green north.

"Does anyone know of their croft?"
our waitress asks, and the pub begins reminiscing
about everyone else, revelling in the past.
"I remember them," a farmer in gumboots says.
"No, Colin Geddes, have ya' not got ears.
It's Begg, not Bate," someone argues.

Another waitress appears at our table,
and the whole pub has forgotten us in their stories.
"The place you're seekin' is on my farm,
but you'll not want to be goin' there
on a night like tonight."

But the sun sets here at eleven and there's
two more hours of northern light, so we go
to a barley field up the road
rimmed with gorse and broom,
wind-flattened and rain-bent,
New World gortex barely helps
as the rain comes up and around, lifting our hoods.
"You can't miss it," she'd said,

"And we're almost there," I say to my wife,
my father's words every time we got lost.
But in this light, every glen

resembles the one we want,
and every grove is tall to a stranger,
until we find the low stone fence,
built of boulders from the nearby sea,
here in the stony and green north
where great sheets of shale
hang like plywood along the pastures.

An iron stile creaks near the empty hole
the ancient tomb has tumbled in.
Branches whip from the low trees,
clustered near the stonepiles of crofts,
all that is left, shadows in the rain.
A good place for a horror movie, I say to the wind,
and then my wife screams.
She touched a tombstone
alive with slugs.

But we've come this far, back across the ocean,
by luck and a memory older than mine,
finding the clues my grandmother left
her father and his and the ones before him.
The clouds have blocked
the setting sun and we are alone with the dead.

"Over here," she shouts, "I've found them."
On my knees, I scrape the stones:
William Begg, Tacksman, born 1759.
Mary Begg born 1763.
Between them an oak sapling sprouts.

I prune the tree with my knife, cut away
the moss, my nails clogged with Scottish mud.

I know this is the last time
anyone will come from North America
and the land will take back the stones
as it has the Tomb at Dunn, as it has them.

For now, I honour my family with my hands
cutting away the grass
and the earth that has begun its work.
And since there are no parish clark's records,
their words end here.

There's nothing more than the clues of our names,
and the walking down cobblestone streets of Wick
and watching the cannon in Stromness harbour
that hailed the Hudson's Bay boats
leaving for the New World.
This was the harbour he sailed from.

Everywhere I see faces like my own
and in Paisley as we take an airport bus
a woman smiles. Later, as the plane lifts
over Glasgow, when it's safe, I know
it's my grandmother's face
and I'm not the first to lose tears over the Atlantic
leaving those streets, those faces of family.

I went to find myself and instead got lost:
returning with a Flemish name, Bruce,
people of the brush,
given to a Scottish hero
and a name favoured by the English nobility
— for their dogs.

Mine a mongrel mix of Nordic and Celtic blood,
from Tuscany and Turkey

and when one of my students mistakes me for a Jew,
I love the holy confusion of the New World
and know why I've always loved the Russian poets
who knew all this.

And I go one more time to the Glenbow,
where the curator holds up the kilt
and the jacket. Like me, my great-great grandfather
a small man with tiny feet.
I'm driven to foolishness and dreams,
poetry and wandering,
and the certainty I sought once
now replaced with the knowing
we are the parts of history,
not always the ones we wish.

IF IT WEREN'T FOR GLEN

The riflepits that day at Batoche,
lying on my stomach,
an imaginary rifle in my hands,
defending the village.
One of Dumont's sharpshooters,
straw in my nostrils,
wind rustling in my ears.
A bead drawn on the steamer,
coming upriver with the Canadian Expeditionary Force.

And there's a cable strung
to bring down the riverboat's stack,
when he gives us the command
to finish the government bastards,
but Riel prays and Dumont's orders never come.

Now there's a museum erected
by the government of Canada
— on what was Métis land.

And if weren't for Glen
the gentle ironist who teaches
rage without raging,
we wouldn't have left the sparkling glass museum
to the glory of Upper Canada

and taken the dirt road twelve miles
to a roofless place under the sky,
wolf willow along the barbed wire fences,
without glass, open to the rain
and sun and wind and cattle
and doubt.

We couldn't have found
in the cow pasture at Fish Creek

the fenced graves of Middleton's men
honouring one battle
the Métis won.

In Glen's museum
history begins, not ends,
and in the pub, uneasy over our beer,
we hear the Métis patois of the ferryman
who pilots the river a dozen times each day
and whose name is Dumont.

CHASING THE TRAIN

Between Toronto and Stratford
on the CN's main line, west of Guelph
where Scottish stonemasons' work lines the track
the country opens up green and stony
and farmers are named Glendinning.

You'll see a border collie, a legless roundabout blur
of black and white,
a solitary Highlander in a sheepless pasture,
chasing the train a full quarter mile
flat-out along the fence.

So strong the urge to work, that twice
each day, she's after the gleaming silver Superliner
hurtling to and from Chicago,
windows full of tourists expecting sheep.

And I'm betting one day, she'll break past
the fences, seize the train by its tail.
Whatever would she do
with eight double-decked silver coloured sheep
if she caught them? But that's quibbling,
for a working dog in a pasture without sheep,
who's been bred for centuries,
she's not wondering at all.

Just bound determined she's going to,
one of these days,
even as she stops at the fence.
Next time, her eyes and tilted tongue say,
as she lets us go, barrelling home.

COMING HOME FROM HOME

Eighteen years in exile —
gone from the Gaelic city of my birth
to the land that sent the men to hunt Riel.

Riel voted by his people
to the Parliament of Canada —
Riel the poet, the prophet —
who prayed to God
when Dumont had the bastards cornered.

Eighteen years still haunted by the ghost of the man
who stepped aside on the word of Macdonald
while Cartier went in Riel's stead.

And a few years later, needing votes
in the country of the Orangeman Scott,
Macdonald sent troops
after a man who trusted him.

(Riel elected three times to Parliament
by his people, went once, signed in and left
before the clerk spotted him.
But that night all Ottawa came to the public gallery.
Riel slipped away fearing for his life.)
A man who loved his country too much to stay away.

Riel of whom my great-great grandfather wrote home
to Emily in Orillia, October 31, 1869
from Pembina, Manitoba:
My dear wife, I'm wrapped in
a buffalo robe, my fingers freezing
we have lost our horses and have been
wandering the prairies for weeks.

The road barricaded ten miles
from here by a hand of half breeds
led by a Jesuit. I'm afraid
we must turn back.

I'm torn for the land I've left,
and come to love the land that kept the bell from Batoche
until three years ago a truck with Saskatchewan plates
driven, some say, by the ghost of Dumont, stole it back
from the Legion Hall — gone forever
in the revenge of Batoche
and I tell you, I had nothing to do with it.

Living in the country of the Orangeman,
and the judge who sentenced him to hang,
I'm still shaken by the memory of Riel, a Catholic,
and how home is a dubious name
for what the heart can't have —
this land where my great-great-grandfather's
son left school, to ride west before the railroad
and take up land at the confluence of the Bow and
Highwood
    — for services rendered in the Rebellion —
but he learned at Guelph and wrote the Dominion's men,
"grazing land," he'd not plow it
and to this day it's unbroken,
cattle companies along the Bow.

But the green Ontario boy couldn't know how
his lush meadow on the best trout stream
in the south-east was a flood plain,
this land that his father
from the stormy northeast of Scotland
where the Norsemen landed

named it after the town of his birth
and the river — Dunbow —
the need to name our place, each other,
this time, this year.

They left me no land
only this diseased Nordic light that blinds me now —
like them, I have wandered
and everywhere is home when home is nowhere
near anywhere anymore.
And the names keep changing —
mine Flemish for people of the brush,
theirs Gaelic for a small people.
Their Highland dancing shoes
fit my tiny feet.

Eighteen years in exile
in the land of the men who hanged Riel
and I move too easily among them
not safe from the memory
knowing that to name us and this place
is to fix us only for an instant
on a map we crossed and
crossed out again
and again.

Leaving the stones of the croft,
the Tomb at Dunn, the graveyard and its markers,
the fallow grass of the ranch and the rutted
cart tracks filled with runoff. And oh,
those letters, if we are lucky,
long after love's hushed
and the lovely letters of their names
keep us coming home from home.

Printed in April 2000 by

ON DEMAND PRINTING INC.

in Longueuil, Quebec